An Angel at Christmas

by Álvaro Correa, LC

Illustrated by Gloria Lorenzo

CIRCLE
PRESS

Translated by Eamonn O'Higgins, LC, from the original Spanish edition, *Navidad con mi Ángel de la Guarda,* © Copyright 2009

First U.S. edition published by Circle Press, a division of Circle Media, Inc.

Illustrations by Gloria Lorenzo

ISBN: 978-1-933271-29-3

PRINTED IN THE UNITED STATES OF AMERICA

5 4 3 2 1

To all members of ECYD and NET

To the families of this year's newborn children

TABLE OF CONTENTS

INTRODUCTION

Christmas is best portrayed in Nativity scenes in Christian homes. At least that's what Jimmy, the hero of this story, thinks. Jimmy is a simple boy with a good heart who lives with his family in a house in the country.

On this particular Christmas Eve, just like every year, he fired a personal message for the Infant Jesus from his slingshot into the sky (and towards heaven). This small and apparently insignificant gesture would be the beginning of a special adventure. The Holy Family thanks him for his prayer and invites him to help them make sure that "the Infant Jesus will be born in the hearts of many people."

Helped by his guardian angel, Jimmy travels halfway around the world to bring some people a special gift – a small figure of the Infant Jesus for their Nativity scene. Each situation describes a particular scene, depicting the holy wishes of each person involved. Jimmy enjoys each visit and only wishes that he could stay longer. Jimmy forms a special bond of friendship with each person who sets out to search for God in his or her life.

This story gives a special place to guardian angels, whose friendship and sympathy bring smiles to children's faces. In fact, it was the angels who first announced the birth of the Savior, and who's to say that our own guardian angels were not also there with them?

Jimmy often talks with his guardian angel and knows that his angel is with him always and helps him by guiding his conscience. The two of them are always chatting together; a sign of the holy devotion Jimmy has had for his angel since he was a very young child.

As you read this story, you also are invited to become a friend of Jimmy's and to ask your own guardian angel to help you travel the world.

Maybe in some real way Jimmy represents all those who try to bring the love of the Infant Jesus to their own families and to many others throughout the world on Christmas Eve.

Álvaro Correa, LC
Christmas 2009

The Stone with a Message

Jimmy pulled back on his slingshot and launched the stone towards the middle of the whitest cloud that he saw in the sky. The stone was as large as a nut, but as it flew off into the white cloud, it became as tiny as the smallest black spot on a Dalmatian dog.

"Come on, fly, fly!" shouted Jimmy at the top of his lungs. Had it not been for the law of gravity, that stone would most surely have penetrated that cloud and broken the windshield of some celestial spaceship. What a scare for the astronauts! In reality, Jimmy's imagination lasted much longer than the stone did in returning to Earth.

It was Christmas Eve. Just like every year, Jimmy, a happy boy who was as restless as a squirrel, used his slingshot to launch a message he had written for the Infant Jesus as far as he could. In fact, the day before he spent all afternoon engraving his message (like an ancient Egyptian scribe) on the brightest and smoothest stone he had chosen from a nearby stream.

Jimmy stood on the balcony of his house and tried to guess where the stone had landed. It was difficult to say, but it was somewhere beyond the garden of his own house, past the road to the village, over a stretch of land, across the stream, and into a thick grove of chestnut trees. The boy fixed his eyes on the unknown point, waved a salute, and put the slingshot in the back pocket of his jeans.

"Did you send the message?" asked his little sister, Sophie, who had just arrived. She was out of breath from having climbed the stairs in a hurry. The answer was more than obvious, as she observed her brother with his hands empty and his "weapon" put away. "Why didn't you wait for me? I wanted to see you do it!"

Why did Sophie want to see her brother launch that stone? It wasn't really out of curiosity, because she had seen him do it hundreds of times, and she knew that Jimmy had the reputation of being the best slingshot shooter among the children of the neighborhood. No, that was not the reason for Sophie's question. It was because Jimmy had told her that if the Infant Jesus were to read his message, something very special would happen. And we know what surprises mean for children.

"How far did the message go?" asked Sophie, gazing into the sky and shading her forehead with her hand.

"Oh, high, very high! It reached the cloud!" said Jimmy, pointing out the large shimmering cloud he had aimed at.

"Did it go through it?"

"Of course! Can't you see the hole in the middle?"

Jimmy's slingshot was not exactly a bazooka. Even so, he really thought the stone had reached the cloud. His heart still beat with the excitement of sending his Christmas message to the Infant Jesus.

The children ran down the stairs two at a time, and their mother – who kept a watchful eye on both of them – told them to be careful.

"Mom, Jimmy sent his message to the Infant Jesus," whispered Sophie in her mother's ear. Their mother smiled and said, "I'm glad. He will be very happy, but remember the Infant Jesus still does not know how to read. It will be his mother, the Virgin Mary, who will read the message to him."

Shortly afterwards, Jimmy raced towards the village on his bike. He wanted to see how all the Christmas preparations were coming along at his friends' houses, in the square, and in the parish church. He planned to get firsthand information from his friends: Tony, the mayor's son; Gerard, the cousin of the toy store owner; Harry, the school principal's son; Mark, the bell-ringer's son; and Nathaniel, the nephew of Father Andrew, the parish priest.

As he arrived at the wooden bridge over the stream, Jimmy stopped his bicycle. Leaning on one leg, he looked towards the forest and again felt sure that he had launched the stone much farther than the previous year. It was a good day, and he wanted to explore a little ways into the forest. He did not think he'd be able to find the stone; in fact, he wanted to be sure that he wouldn't find it so he could be sure that heaven had received his message.

He steered his bike away from the road, leaving the village behind. Just after the bridge, there was a path that led into the forest. It was covered with soft leaves. Jimmy went forward along the path. He came to a small incline and got off his bike, leaning it against a tree (the same tree that he and his friends had tied some rope to a few days before). He glanced back to see where his house was so he could figure out the flight of the stone (and his message).

Jimmy began to hum a Christmas carol. The sun shone between the branches, and several small birds flew around happily. He stopped for a moment to see two squirrels chasing each other around an old oak tree. Jimmy recognized them as "Romeo and Juliet"; at least that's what he named them the first time he had seen them, and ever since he liked to bring them nuts and cookies. The squirrels paused a moment and looked at him. The boy put his hand in his pocket, dug down deep, and managed to find two peanuts. It was a tasty snack for the two small creatures.

Jimmy followed the path and came to a clearing. He thought that his message could have landed there. He bent down and began to search the ground, which was entirely covered with leaves, branches, and mushrooms. A few sluggish snails were out, moving slowly along.

Just then, he heard a soft melody, the musical notes of a sweet-sounding flute, which sounded even more beautiful in contrast to the silence of the forest. Jimmy turned to see who was playing the flute and saw a young man dressed in white coming toward him. The young man stopped playing the flute and bowed to greet him.

The Nativity Cave

"**D**o you like the sound of my flute?" asked the young man, whose voice also sounded like a musical instrument. "Yes, I do," answered Jimmy somewhat timidly, looking at the young man with interest. To Jimmy, the young man seemed to be made of bright light, and his flowing robes swayed in a breeze that Jimmy did not feel.

"Don't be afraid, Jimmy."

In fact, Jimmy did not feel afraid, but instead felt a strange admiration for this young man. "Who are you?" he asked him.

The young man smiled with the understanding that a friend has when he shows up unexpectedly without being recognized. "Maybe I should ask the first question."

Jimmy nodded his head in agreement and put his curiosity on hold. Yes, it was probably better to know the reason for this meeting. Maybe the young man was there on behalf of someone else, and it would be more appropriate to ask about that person. "What do you want to ask me? You seem to know more than I do."

The young man looked pleased on hearing these humble words, and taking a step forward, asked him, "Jimmy, do you want to know about what you wrote so lovingly to the Infant Jesus?"

The boy closed his eyes and thought back to the previous afternoon, remembering the stone, which turned around in his mind like a small world. The words he had written shone in a bright gold color. The image in his mind was so colorful and bright that for a moment he doubted it was just a memory. He opened his eyes again and realized that the young man was still there in front of him. No, it was not his imagination.

"So, your silence means yes?" asked the young man.

"Yes," answered Jimmy.

As Jimmy's lips pronounced that important word "yes," suddenly he too felt the breeze that moved the young man's robes. It was like a soft touch that began to surround his body. The young man took him by the hand, and together they took off flying. It was a feeling that Jimmy had only dreamed of in his imagination. In an instant, they were both in the middle of the friendly white cloud. But just as Jimmy tried to touch it, they began a fast descent, like an eagle. Strangely, the boy's stomach did not turn inside out, like on a roller coaster. Instead, it was just the opposite – the wind continued to swirl gently around them as if they were traveling in an air-conditioned bubble. Jimmy began to think that the young man moved around from place to place wrapped up in a little piece of heaven.

They landed in an open field near some small cottages that looked like they had been recently painted. Although Jimmy wanted to know exactly where they were, he had another question in mind.

"Hey, you're an angel, right? What's your name, or are you just called 'Angel'?"

"Yes, I am an angel. I have not told you my name because I like what you call me."

"Oh, you mean my little 'angel buddy'?" Jimmy answered, suddenly realizing that the young man was his guardian angel.

The difference between an angel and a little "angel buddy" was not really a question of size. What Jimmy referred to as angels were those images he had seen in books and illustrated Bibles and paintings in the parish church. But "angel buddy" was reserved only for his guardian angel, as in the daily prayer: "Angel of God, my guardian dear…"

Jimmy was happy and gave the angel a hug. What's it like to hug an angel? You'll have to ask Jimmy someday.

"Wow, I thought that you would be more my size. How would I have recognized you?"

"Yes, Jimmy, I appear a little older to be able to help you. Anyway, I can tell you that angels don't have either age or size. Right now you are seeing the shape God gave me to meet you."

Jimmy understood, but not entirely. He was eleven years old, and he saw everything as good because he accepted everything with love.

His "angel buddy" then showed him an open cave at the foot of a mountain. The boy was surprised, because he did not remember ever seeing a cave near his house.

"Jimmy, we're here at the Nativity cave. They are waiting for us."

"What Can I Do?"

Holding onto the angel's hand and flying through the air with him had been a wonderful experience, but it had been almost too much for Jimmy. The angel had flown at full speed – *Too fast,* Jimmy thought. The boy wondered if it was necessary to travel at that speed to arrive on time in Bethlehem.

As they walked towards the entrance to the cave, they met a flock of sheep. Jimmy spotted one small lamb that was bleating woefully.

"What's wrong with that lamb?" Jimmy bent down and picked the little animal up. It was as soft and light as a pillow. The lamb seemed to rest easily in Jimmy's arms, although its legs still trembled a little.

As soon as they entered the cave, they found Mary and Joseph and the Infant Jesus in the manger. Jimmy quietly knelt down. Instinctively he closed his eyes, because inside the shadowy cave there was an atmosphere of silence and prayer.

The angel whispered something to Jimmy in the soft voice that he always used to give some good advice or suggest a good action.

"Come closer, and adore the Infant Jesus."

Obediently, Jimmy set the lamb on the ground and straightened up. His heart beat like a drum, and he felt his cheeks flush. Just then, the Virgin Mary approached him and offered him her hand.

"What a pleasure to see you, Jimmy!" she said.

"Do you know me?" Jimmy asked.

The Virgin Mary gazed on him with love and leaned over to kiss him. Then she said, "I know each one of my children." Jimmy

kissed the Virgin Mary, and St. Joseph as well, and he gazed at the newborn baby. How beautiful and tiny he was!

It had been only two days since Jimmy had received the holy Eucharist at Sunday Mass. Now that Jimmy saw the Infant Jesus with his own eyes, he wondered even more at the mystery of God hidden in the white host. There, in front of the Infant Jesus, everything was quiet, as quiet and solemn as the inside of some great cathedral.

The Virgin Mary gave Jimmy a hug, and then she took the Infant Jesus delicately in her arms, kissed him, and presented him to Jimmy. Jimmy gave the infant a kiss, noticing how a small smile appeared on the tiny lips of the newborn baby.

Jimmy had heard that a number of shepherds came to adore the Infant Jesus after he was born, but he did not see them anywhere.

They have most likely already come and gone – or maybe my angel buddy has brought me here before they arrived, thought Jimmy. But then the Virgin Mary spoke to him.

"My child, I was very happy to read the message you sent to my Infant Jesus."

"Did you like it?"

"Yes! I felt your heart beat with joy. You know that every Christmas my infant son comes again into the world to beg for a place in the hearts of all men and women. You can imagine his joy when a friend receives him with love."

"I only wrote a few words…"

Just then, St. Joseph put his hand into an old leather bag and took out the stone that Jimmy had launched with his slingshot. "You have great aim and strength, boy! You almost hurt our donkey!"

Everyone laughed as he showed the stone again to the Virgin Mary, who held the infant in her arms. As St. Joseph held the stone up to her eyes, the Virgin Mary read out loud the words that Jimmy had written. As the Virgin Mary moved her lips, Jimmy repeated softly the same words: "I want you to be born in many hearts."

St. Joseph looked at Jimmy and graciously nodded his approval. He then put the stone back in the bag, but it seemed to Jimmy that the stone did not reach the bottom of the bag. The humble carpenter saw his surprise and said, "This bag? It has no weight." And he handed it to Jimmy for a moment. Jimmy bounced it in his hands as though it were a ping-pong ball.

"Wow, it's weightless! But what about my stone?"

"Ah, the stone! Do you mean this year's stone, or the stones from previous years, which were even heavier? They're all here. And if you put your hand into the bag, you will draw out the letters of millions of children that have been sent to the Infant Jesus – so many gifts that have been left at the Nativity scenes in parishes, toys that they have given him for centuries, medals given to him in thanksgiving for favors received, and many, many other gifts and prayers. Do you know the secret of why the bag weighs so little?"

"No, why?"

St. Joseph leaned down to Jimmy and whispered, "I keep here only what is given to the Infant Jesus with love."

Jimmy felt a special joy running through him, knowing that all his messages were there in the bag. Then he said, "My angel buddy brought me here because I told him that I wanted to start doing what I wrote to the Infant Jesus." Jimmy looked into the beautiful eyes of the Virgin Mary and put himself at her service. "What would you like me to do?"

St. Joseph took the Virgin Mary's hand and, caressing the baby, said, "Jimmy, I was told in dreams what I had to do when Mary agreed to be the Mother of God, after Archangel Gabriel visited her. I'm happy now to tell you (and not in a dream!) that the Infant Jesus, Mary, my dear wife, and I want to give you a special task."

"What? What can I do so that the Infant Jesus is born in many hearts?"

"It's something simple, as all of God's works are, but it will have a lasting effect. You see, Jimmy, your guardian angel…"

"My angel buddy?"

"Yes, your little angel buddy will bring you to visit some families.

And you can travel more slowly this time, if you like, so you can enjoy the journey. All you have to do is give the families a little image of the Infant Jesus for the Nativity scenes in their homes this Christmas."

"That's all?"

"Yes. It will be easy for you, but remember that the hearts of men and women are prepared from within by love. You see, we are asking you to knock on the door of these homes so that we can enter in. Now do you understand?"

Jimmy did understand, and he answered by nodding his head. It was not surprising that the Infant Jesus, at the very moment Jimmy accepted out of love for him, opened his eyes and looked at Jimmy for a few moments. All the happiness of Christmas suddenly flooded Jimmy's pure heart. The boy with the slingshot, who had arrived at the cave led by an angel, now wanted to travel the whole world, on foot if necessary, to announce that love had been born for the hearts of all.

A Little Girl with a Big Smile

Jimmy and his guardian angel left the cave immediately. It was just as well that they did, because at the entrance they ran into a crowd of shepherds – the ones Jimmy had been looking for.

"Do you realize the privilege that the Virgin Mary and St. Joseph have given you?" the angel asked. "You met them personally, and all by yourself!"

"Yes, and I think I know why," Jimmy answered. "They are going to ask the shepherds for something different. The shepherds can't leave their sheep to go traveling around the world like us, right?"

"Maybe not. Instead, the shepherds' task will be to welcome the Holy Family on Christmas night and announce the Savior's birth to the neighboring villages. But, really, if it were necessary, their guardian angels could bring the shepherds and their flocks around the entire world. Do you believe that?"

"No way, angel buddy! Just kidding; I do believe it. All I was saying –"

"Don't worry; I understand." The angel took his hand, and looking at a star that beamed brightly just then, asked him, "Ready?"

They flew off as fast as lightning. The countryside they passed was beautiful, and this time Jimmy could actually enjoy the sights. In the distance, there was a mountain range completely covered with snow, and the angel flew towards it at a steep angle. Not even the finest eagle could have imitated the angel's dexterity in swerving in and out between the peaks. A high mountain made it necessary for them to fly almost straight up. The angel stopped on the peak of the mountain, and they both placed their feet on a cushion of snow.

"Do you see the villages in this valley? We're heading for the one right in the middle."

"Where?"

The angel pointed out a group of houses clustered around a parish church, with the church steeple standing out like a large needle.

"Which house are we going to?"

"The one right in front of the post office."

The angel stretched out his arm and pointed towards the house. A ray of light was shining from his finger, and it seemed like part of the angel himself. Jimmy's eyes opened wide, and he smiled in wonder.

"Angel buddy, can you light up everything like a lamp?"

"Sure, it's easy. But do you know what's difficult even for an angel?"

"What?"

"It's hard for us to speak with heavenly power, to speak with all of God's wisdom and love to men and women who don't want to listen to us."

Jimmy thought about this, as if making a small examination of his own conscience. Then he said, "Angel buddy, if I have ever…"

"No, I don't mean you, Jimmy. You do listen to me. If not, would we be here? Look, right now you are going to go into a house, and you have to give all your love to the people you meet there. Remember that you are bringing them a gift that the Infant Jesus is sending them. Let's go!"

They made their descent by following the ray of light that led to the house. Suddenly, Jimmy found himself alone in front of the entrance to the house, with the figure of the Infant Jesus in his hands.

"Angel buddy!" the boy shouted. He didn't hear an answer; he only felt an encouraging hand on his back. Even though he didn't see anyone, he felt reassured, knowing that his angel was with him as usual – that is, invisibly.

He knocked on the door, and a boy of his own age opened it.

"Hi! Are you looking for someone?"

Jimmy didn't know what to say, but he spoke words that seemed to come from his heart.

"Yes… I'd like to see your family."

"My family? Well, then, come on in."

It was pleasant for Jimmy to go into a house in the valley, and as he did, he heard music from a piano that a young girl with long blond hair was playing. In the background, a fire crackled in the fireplace in a playful way. A young woman appeared from the kitchen.

"Mom," her son said to her, "this boy knocked at the door and said that he has come to see us."

The young mother was surprised to see the unknown boy with a figure of the Infant Jesus in his hands. "What's your name? What can we do for you?"

By this time, the girl had stopped playing the piano, and the fireplace lit up the faces of everyone that came to see who had arrived. There were the parents, the girl at the piano, the boy who had opened the door, and another small child.

"Hi, I'm Jimmy, and…"

What am I going to tell them? Jimmy thought to himself, worrying just a little. At that moment, he saw that the ray of light coming from the angel's finger was still shining; it pointed to a bed through the half-open door of another room.

"…I just came to give this figure of the Infant Jesus to the boy there in the bed."

Jimmy's words, spoken firmly and enthusiastically, filled everyone with joyful surprise. The little toddler cried out at the top of his small voice, "It's not a boy! She's called Jessica!"

The boy who had opened the door for Jimmy put his arm around Jimmy and said: "I'm Nicolas. Do you want to meet our new little sister?"

Nicolas gently guided Jimmy towards the room. "She was baptized last month, and her name is Jessica. She's a little girl that God has given us. We adopted her because she's an orphan and she's sick. We all love her."

As Jimmy entered the room, he realized that the angel's ray of light had vanished. The young mother lit a funnel-shaped lantern that shone its light up to the ceiling. Its pale yellow color was both warm and inviting.

Everyone gathered around the bed, leaving room for Jimmy, who was the last to arrive with his new friend Nicolas. Then he saw Jessica, a beautiful little girl, asleep and covered with a rose-colored handmade blanket. She was three or four years old. Jimmy did not ask why she was sick because he didn't think it was necessary for him to know. It was her adopted family's love that would be with her as long as she lived. This little girl suffered from a serious illness that made it impossible for her to see or speak.

"Jimmy, isn't my sister beautiful?" asked the toddler.

"She's precious," answered Jimmy, as he leaned over to kiss her cheek and place the statue of the Infant Jesus beside her.

None of the children knew that the doctor who was taking care of Jessica had warned the parents of the possibility of a serious re-

lapse. The girl was very weak, and it was not certain that she would see the new year. But the children had guessed something from their parents' concerned eyes, and they all knew that the situation was serious. They all increased their love and care for this "little flower" who had come into their home.

Everyone felt both hope and concern as they saw the little girl open her beautiful dark eyes. Her new family covered her with kisses and hugs. It was only Jimmy who spoke.

"Jessica, the Infant Jesus has come to visit you," he said, and they were all filled with wonder to see the girl slowly stretch out her arm with great effort and touch the statue of the Infant Jesus. Her smile was so evident that immediately her mother placed the Infant Jesus on her chest.

"Thank you, Jimmy," the mother said. "You have brought us the Christmas that we wanted to share together as a family. Here we all are with the Infant Jesus and Jessica. Thank you very much."

Nicolas once again put his arm on Jimmy's shoulder. It was

amazing – Jimmy had never made friends that quickly with anyone before. He took his time making friends and usually had to play with someone for a while to see if he would be a good friend. Then Jimmy said: "I would like to stay a little longer, but I'm in a hurry."

"What are you going to do now?" Nicolas asked.

"I have to visit other families."

"Do you want me to go with you?"

"Well, I don't know if..."

Nicolas' mother interrupted before Jimmy could continue. "I think Jimmy means that he will come again another day."

Jimmy nodded his head in agreement, but he was not sure he would be able to. He gave his friend a hug, kissed Jessica again, and said good-bye to everyone. As they accompanied Jimmy to the front door, they saw that he had come alone. It seemed strange to all of them except, obviously, to Jimmy, who waved good-bye and began to run after a ray of light that only he saw, one that led him a little beyond the post office, where his angel buddy was waiting for him.

The Unhappy Carpenter

The guardian angel had prepared a snack for Jimmy. They sat down on a park bench that was lit up by lampposts. Although there was snow all around, Jimmy did not feel cold because he still enjoyed staying within the little piece of heaven that surrounded his angel friend.

"I hope you like cupcakes, Jimmy."

"They're delicious! Do you want one?"

"No thanks. You like them better. They are all for you."

"Wow! Do angels eat things?"

"You're very curious, Jimmy. Angels don't need to eat cupcakes because the only hunger we have is for the love of God, and heaven is full of God's love. How can I explain it? It's as though a mouse lived in the biggest cheese factory in the world and the owner was his best friend. It's not exactly like that, but that gives you an idea."

Jimmy ate the last of the cupcakes as he listened to the angel. He appreciated the angel's effort to explain in simple language something so hard to understand.

"Thanks, angel buddy, for all your kindness to me," he said.

In a few moments they were again in flight. Jimmy saw a large lake dotted with small sailboats.

"Look, they seem like toys!"

The angel took just a quick glance and then veered towards the east. They passed over a forest of pine trees that covered a mountain range. The forest seemed endless. Soon, however, they came to a series of red roofs. The angel slowed down to just one mile an hour, and as they flew on he told Jimmy about the next visit.

"We're here, Jimmy! As you can see, we are in a village surrounded by thick forests. In this village, there are as many carpenters as trees, but there is one carpenter in particular who needs a visit from you. I have to warn you, he is quite elderly and unhappy, but I'm sure you will know how to make him smile."

"Is he a grouch?"

"I didn't want to say it like that, but you're exactly right."

"Should I be scared?"

"Don't worry; this old man has never harmed a fly. It's just that he gets mad at everyone."

The angel gave Jimmy the statue of the Infant Jesus wrapped in a white handkerchief and left him standing in a workshop. The smell of freshly cut wood filled his lungs. Jimmy noticed a series of wooden carvings that were all lined up carefully on shelves. The old man might have the worst of tempers, but he also had a very special talent. A couple of squirrels carved out of wood reminded Jimmy of his own little mascots, Romeo and Juliet.

The boy walked towards the sound of someone hammering some wood. Yes, a few feet away there was a tall man with broad shoulders and white hair. He had strong hands that seemed to envelop the tools he was using. His hands were as big as baseball gloves. Jimmy swallowed nervously and, kissing the statue of the Infant Jesus, cleared his throat. The carpenter did not hear. Then Jimmy did something that could have gotten him in trouble – he whistled. The man's arms shot up in surprise, and the hammer flew through the air and fell loudly on a pile of wood.

"What in heaven's name was that?" he shouted. Turning around, he stood one step away from Jimmy, just as Goliath long ago stood in front of young David.

"Hi… It was me."

"So! It was you! And what are you doing here, you little bit of a man?"

That phrase, "little bit of a man," did not sit well with Jimmy, and like a cat showing its claws for the first time, he answered, "If

I'm a bit…then you're a chunk of a man!"

The man roared with laughter, which seemed to ease the tension.

"Okay, lad, tell me what you want, and then leave me in peace."

"Leave you in peace? Look, if you're in a hurry to have me leave, then you should know that I was in an even bigger hurry to get here."

The man furrowed his eyebrows. "And where did you come from?"

"Well…" Jimmy didn't really know what to say. "Well, my house is hours away by flying."

Another peal of laughter rang out, louder than the recent hammer blows.

"What stories you're telling now! What airport did you land at? The toy airport in the shop, or did you land in a stable?"

Jimmy remembered that his angel buddy had told him that

he would be able to make this man smile, but Jimmy didn't think that meant he'd get such a mocking laugh. Maybe he was doing something wrong. But just then he saw his angel's face smiling at him and, turning around, saw him kissing a series of carvings of the Infant Jesus that were on a table at the end of the workshop. Jimmy continued the conversation by saying, "You're laughing because you don't understand what I've just said, but that doesn't matter."

"So you're calling me a fool now?"

Jimmy decided to ignore this comment and changed the subject. "Can I ask you a favor?"

"A favor?"

"Yes, only one."

"What is it?"

"A friend told me that you were the best carpenter in town, and I would like to know if you have any statues of the Infant Jesus."

"Of course I do!"

The fact that (apparently) they had started talking business changed the tone of the conversation. The old man turned around and began to walk among his tables and shelves. For a moment Jimmy thought of him as a grumpy bear that changed into a playful creature when given a few pieces of honey candy – that is, if the people who visited him just talked about buying his carvings and left it at that. They went towards the back of the workshop, and there on a table was a collection of carvings of the Infant Jesus.

"Look, you can see all the statues of the Infant Jesus. It's a big collection of different sizes, different types of wood…" The carpenter talked on and on; he gave a mini lesson on each figure that he picked up in his huge hands. After quite some time, Jimmy interrupted him. "I'm sorry –"

"What! You don't like them?"

"I do like them! I would like to have one of my own. I just wonder why you have so many and why they are all on this table away from all the other statues."

The old carpenter, who at first had been angry, and then had been ready to do business, now let his eyes drop to the ground, as if carrying something sad in his heart that he found hard to bear.

"Do you want to know why? No one asks me because everyone knows… or because they're scared of me."

"Well, I'm not, and I want to know."

"What's your name, boy?"

Jimmy was happy that the old man had asked him his name. It was the same difference between "angel" and "angel buddy." By just saying his name, he would change from "boy" to "Jimmy, his friend."

Spontaneously, before telling the man his name, he put out his hand, not afraid to see it disappear in the carpenter's own huge hands. "My name is Jimmy. Pleased to meet you."

"The pleasure's mine, Jimmy. I'm Henry. They say I'm mean, but what can I do? I'm like a pine tree that can't change itself into an oak tree."

This was a good carpenter's explanation, and Jimmy caught on immediately.

"Oh, don't worry. Each one of us is made of a different wood, but we all have our own scent, and we can all be carved into shape."

"Exactly, my young man." It was plain to see that Henry agreed with what Jimmy said, and he continued: "Sit down there. You asked me about the Infant Jesus carvings. Well, the villagers say that my little boy, the most wonderful little boy that ever existed…"

Henry found a sturdy chair and sat down. His voice began to tremble, and his eyes filled with tears. He pulled out a handkerchief that seemed to Jimmy to be as big as a sheet, and he wiped his face.

"…My little boy left me forever one Christmas night, and I have never gotten over it. I went off into the forest, living in the wild. I hid myself from my wife and my other boys, even though they called out for me day and night in the forest. You can't imagine how angry I was with myself, and with everyone, even with heaven. One day I felt that I had calmed down, and I came back home. I didn't have any more tears left, but I didn't have any smiles to offer anyone either."

"Can I ask a question?"

"Go ahead. You don't need to ask my permission."

"Well, then... What does that very sad story have to do with these carvings?"

"The villagers all know."

"Yes, you said that, but I don't."

Henry covered his face with his hands and was silent. Jimmy could hear him breathing. "Well, since my boy died at Christmas... Well, I thought at first that – I know it's wrong to say this – it was a punishment for me, but when I came back to the village Christmas was coming again, and I thought that maybe the good Lord had forgotten about me, but I was never sure."

Jimmy stood up and put his hand on Henry's shoulder. "Do you know that I've brought you a gift?"

"A gift? Oh, no. Forget it, Jimmy. I have never accepted a gift from anyone since that night."

Jimmy saw a flicker of that old temper flare up in Henry's eyes again. The poor man was like a volcano ready to throw out red-hot lava. The temperature was rising fast, so he quickly gave the old man the figure wrapped in the white handkerchief. Henry hesitated, but he didn't refuse it.

The grace of God always arrives in really difficult moments, and that's how it was with Henry. He took the gift, and with great care, he opened the handkerchief. As he looked at the statue of the Infant Jesus, his eyes opened so wide that Jimmy was worried. *What had happened?* Jimmy wondered.

"Jimmy! Don't you see?"

Without another word, Henry clasped the figure to his chest, overcome with emotion. "Look at his face! Look at those eyes!"

Jimmy looked at the figure cradled in Henry's arms, but he didn't see anything special, except for its outstanding beauty.

"Don't you see?"

"If you would just tell me…"

"It's the face of my son!"

Yes, indeed, the Infant Jesus had the face of Henry's son! Jimmy would never have imagined it, and he could only wonder at the kindness of the Holy Family's gift. Henry continued to clutch and kiss the statue.

Then Jimmy's angel buddy appeared to him beside a wooden statue of an angel that looked a lot like Jimmy's angel. How funny! The boy smiled.

"Are you as happy as I am?" asked the carpenter.

"If you're happy, I'm double-happy!"

"Well, enjoy it, my boy, because I'm running home to put my own boy, my own Infant Jesus, in the Nativity scene. Then I'm going to wake up my wife – she'll be so surprised! What a Christmas we're going to have!"

"I'm so happy for you and your family!"

"Wait – who gave you the statue?"

Jimmy just kept looking at him, smiling from ear to ear. Henry began to smile, tentatively at first, then more and more widely.

"That's our secret, Mr. Henry, sir. I can tell you that your Christmas will be just as special as mine."

"You know something? I haven't smiled since that day… Now I see that my love for my own little boy and for the Infant Jesus are one and the same."

Jimmy saw his angel buddy again, and this time the angel was touching up the pinewood statue that was on the workbench. When his angel buddy had finished his work and drew back his hand, Jimmy was amazed to see that the statue was identical to his angel buddy. What a great little piece of angelical creativity! Is there any other carpenter in the world who could claim to have a carving done by a real angel?

Jimmy said good-bye, taking a figure of the Infant Jesus as a gift from Henry; it was the best one in the workshop. Jimmy gave him a hug and whispered in his ear, "Run home now, but tomorrow when you come back, look for the carving of the angel that you were working on…"

"What? Do you want to take it with you?"

"No, no… It will be another surprise for you."

As he left the carpenter's workplace, Jimmy showed the statue to his guardian angel. "What will I do with it? Can I take it with me?"

"Of course. I'll take care of it while we fly because it means something special to you."

They were ready to take off, but the angel wanted one last look below. "Look, there goes Henry!" Jimmy said, pointing to his friend who was running as quickly as a deer towards his house.

The old carpenter had not smiled so much since his son had died, and neither had he run so fast. What was clear to the old man was that the loving presence of the Infant Jesus had always been there with him, only now he knew it.

Christmas at Emily's House

The next route was really a spectacular one that included crossing an ocean. The guardian angel flew at full speed, and Jimmy felt like he had turned into a ray of light.

"Wow! Awesome!"

"Is my passenger enjoying himself?"

"Yes!"

The angel began to imitate the announcement one hears on planes, which (only the good Lord knows why) always seems to sound the same every time and in every plane: "Hello passenger, the captain and crew wish to inform you that we are now flying over the Atlantic at a speed of…well…lightning speed. Our final destination will be the large house of a special family. There is a mother and father with a girl about your age and two small children. Up until now, Christmas has been just one more party of the many parties they have. What's different this year is that Emily (that's the girl's name) has asked her parents to put a Nativity scene in their home. It has been a bit of an issue because her parents don't want it. The girl's prayer has touched the heart of the Virgin Mary, and she is asking you, dear passenger, to help her. We will be entering through a window of the house in three seconds: one, two, three…"

And, as quick as lightning, Jimmy found himself in the living room of a large mansion. There seemed to be no one there, and Jimmy looked around him, taking in the fancy home that was as big as a palace. His eyes gazed at a beautiful portrait of the family hanging over the fireplace. He saw the girl's face, and she looked like a princess. The carpet Jimmy felt beneath him was thick and cushioned; he felt like he was walking on a featherbed.

Just then he heard a noise. Quickly and quietly (the carpet muffled any sound from his feet), he made his way to the far end of the room, crossed a hall, and came to a wide staircase. The staircase was made of marble with a golden banister. He heard another noise and climbed the stairs, reaching another passageway that led to a lot of rooms.

The door of the last room was partially open. Jimmy walked towards the room, his heart beating loudly, perhaps because of the swift change of scene from the carpenter's humble workshop to this fairy-tale mansion. He stopped in front of the door and began looking for the figure of the Infant Jesus. He didn't have it! He began to get nervous.

"Psst! Jimmy!" It was his guardian angel.

"Just in time! Where's the statue?"

"I'm sorry I didn't tell you before. You know, we were in such a hurry! Look, you don't have to give a statue because…"

And the angel whispered the explanation to Jimmy as he listened intently, nodding his head in agreement.

"And now you see why Emily is expecting you."

Jimmy took a step forward, but stopped and turned to the angel with a puzzled expression. He said, "Excuse me for saying this, but you always say that 'everyone is expecting me,' and what really happens is that no one seems to know that I'm showing up."

The angel smiled, and Jimmy realized the rudeness of what he had just said. He regretted saying more than he should have.

"I'm sorry, angel buddy; I shouldn't have said that."

"Don't worry. Maybe I should have said: 'Everyone *is* expecting you, although they don't know it yet.'"

At that moment, the door opened suddenly, and Jimmy found himself in front of the girl. The angel disappeared. The children looked at each other as if they were school friends meeting at recess.

"Hi, Emily."

"Hi..."

"My name is Jimmy."

"Are you one of my brothers' friends?"

"No… well, yes…"

They heard someone answering the phone, and Jimmy quickly went into Emily's room. She was frightened and said, "What are you doing?"

Jimmy motioned to her to keep quiet and come into the room. The girl was not convinced; she slammed the door, and ran off.

Oh no! sighed Jimmy. He felt for the wall and slid down it until he was sitting on the floor with his hands covering his face. "Angel buddy! What am I supposed to do now?" There was no reply. A minute passed, but to Jimmy it seemed like an eternity. He remembered how he felt when his dad had caught him on his bicycle when he should have been doing something else.

He jumped when he heard a knock on the door. He put his head further between his knees and wrapped himself in his arms, noticing that the door began to open slowly.

"Are you still there?" the girl asked him in a quiet voice.

Jimmy gasped in relief. "Of course I am! Did you think I would run after you?"

The girl came in and closed the door. "I'm sorry, but I don't know you."

"I told you my name is Jimmy."

"So what? You could be called Freddie, too."

The girl smiled when she realized that Jimmy was good-natured and also had the courage to stay in the room, knowing the "risk" he was taking. The fact that the girl had come back was perhaps due to her own guardian angel.

Jimmy stood up and began carrying out his mission. "Emily, I'm sorry for arriving the way I did, and also for not having the time to explain why I'm here in your house without knocking on the door, and why I'm in your room without your permission."

"Yes, it's all very strange," answered the girl, "but at least tell me why you're here."

"Of course; that's what I want to tell you."

The girl sat down on a huge blue ball that turned out to be a seat, and she invited Jimmy to do the same on a red ball.

"Emily, I know that you want to put a Nativity scene of the Infant Jesus here in your house, but your parents won't let you."

"How do you know that?"

"Wait – if I start answering all your questions we will be here for hours!"

"But I want to know! Do you think it's just normal that someone says what you're thinking and saying without having told him? Wouldn't you be curious?"

"Well, okay. Let's make a deal."

"What kind of a deal?"

Jimmy stood up, and the girl watched as he walked around the room and looked out the window as he answered. "The deal is this: I will tell you if you do not ask me any more questions."

"Okay, if that's how you want it."

It has been said that children make friends quickly; in any case, that's how it was with Jimmy and Emily. In less than five minutes they had met, parted company, and been reconciled – and, above all, they had come to an agreement! Next they began a conversation that would greatly encourage Emily.

"Do you know why your parents don't want to put the Nativity scene with the Infant Jesus here in your house? Your house is very impressive, by the way," said Jimmy.

"Well, my mom would. It's Dad who never allowed us to."

"And what did he say?"

"That it's not necessary."

"That it's not necessary?"

"Yes, that's all…" and Emily repeated the phrase: "It's not necessary."

"Wow!"

"Wow what?"

"Nothing – it's just that I thought you were up against some type of dictator or something."

"Well, what do you think?"

"I don't know… It seems like your dad's soul has a slight fever, and we're going to give him his medicine."

Emily was a little confused because she didn't know about Jimmy's contact with his guardian angel and even less about the special mission given to him by the Holy Family. But, above all (and this is worth noting), she trusted Jimmy. Jimmy continued: "Emily, I need you to bring me to the attic."

"What are you going to do? If my parents find out, they will be mad at me."

Jimmy, who wanted to honor his deal with Emily, gave her a partial explanation. "Emily, I'm here because I made a promise to the Infant Jesus, and he took it seriously. Can you remember if you have asked him for something, or if you promised him something?"

Emily looked upwards with her blue eyes, and her face lit up as she remembered. "Yes! I've asked for and promised so many things to the Infant Jesus and the Virgin Mary!"

"Well, they sent me here to help you, and going to the attic is part of the answer to your prayer."

It was then that the mystery of Christmas filled Emily's soul, just like a ray of light cuts through the thickest of clouds. "Let's go!" she answered, and they left the room, both of them determined but proceeding with care. At the end of the hall, there was a flight of stairs that led directly to the attic. Emily turned on the light, and there in front of them was a pile of odds and ends – boxes, files, old pictures, lampshades, and books. Jimmy made his way through the stacks of chairs, and then…

"Here it is!" he shouted enthusiastically.

"What have you found? Is it the medicine for Dad?"

"Exactly, but let me see if it's like my angel buddy told me."

"Angel buddy?"

"Yes…um, he's a friend. He brought me here."

"Who is he? *Where* is he?"

Jimmy looked at Emily, her eyes shining with the goodness and simplicity of her soul. The boy would have liked to explain in detail, but he didn't think he could describe an angel. Even so, he was certain that she could capture some idea of what he meant. He said, "He's here with us, along with your own guardian angel."

Emily nodded. She bent down to help Jimmy lift a trunk. They put it on a table.

"Jimmy, I wonder what's inside?"

"Let's see."

The trunk was locked, but Jimmy wasn't worried. He put his hand in his pocket and took out a key. Emily was surprised. "You have the key?" It was heartwarming to see the amazed look on Emily's face. Jimmy simply told her how it was all part of this mysterious adventure. "Just before I met you at the door of your room, my angel buddy put the key in my pocket." The key fit the lock, and Jimmy opened the trunk. The contents inside were visible for the first time in many years.

"Here, take it," said Jimmy to the girl. She carefully lifted out a beautiful statue of the Infant Jesus. She was filled with wonder. She kissed the statue and gave it to Jimmy, who also kissed it, remembering his recent visit to the real Nativity cave.

Jimmy went on: "Emily, this is going to be a special Christmas for you and your family. Now, while your father is not here, you have some time to prepare the Nativity scene in the living room with the help of your mom and your brothers. When your dad arrives, give him the biggest hug you can and take him by the hand to see the Nativity scene. You can tell him that this statue is the one he received as a gift when he was an altar boy – when he was just about your age.

"As time went on, unfortunately, his faith and friendship with the Infant Jesus began to weaken, until he thought that the Nativity scene was unnecessary at Christmas. The Infant Jesus' plan (which never fails) is to enter into his heart as he did the first time, and that is what the Infant Jesus knows how to do better than anyone else."

As Jimmy spoke, Emily took the statue from him and listened with a deep feeling of gratitude. A tear ran down her cheek. The boy wiped it away gently with his hand.

"I don't know how to thank you, Jimmy."

"Me? No, not me – thank the Infant Jesus. I can tell you that he is the most loving person who has ever lived and who still lives."

"Have you actually seen him?"

Jimmy answered with a smile, nodded his head, and kissed the Infant Jesus good-bye.

"Emily, there's not much time. Go and prepare this first real Christmas in your house, the first of many that you will celebrate with your parents and brothers. You will never forget this Christmas, because you will see your dad become a child at heart again."

The girl walked towards the door, but then turned around and ran back to kiss Jimmy on the cheek. Jimmy turned as red as a lobster. Emily headed for the door and again stopped to look back, but Jimmy was no longer there. There was only the open trunk lit up by a ray of light that shone through the window shutters.

The Missionary and the Leopard

How happy Jimmy was to have visited Jessica, Henry, and Emily! Even so, he was sad not to have been able to stay longer with each one because he now considered them his friends.

"Angel buddy, will I ever see them again?"

"Maybe. The world is a small place," the angel replied.

"You can't imagine how much I would like to!"

"Jimmy, the most important thing is that you have knocked on the door of their homes to make way for the Holy Family to enter in, and you have helped the Infant Jesus to be born in their hearts this Christmas."

"You're right. That was my promise. And now where are we off to?"

The boy did not realize that his guardian angel was heading toward the other side of the world. They had flown over lakes and deserts, forests and cities, canyons and prairies. His angel answered: "Do you like guessing games?"

"Sure I do!"

"Well, I'm not very good, because angels don't play them, but let me give you three words. Choose the one that describes where you think we're going."

"Okay. What are they?"

"The first is 'chalice.' The second is 'volcano,' and the third is 'monument.'"

Jimmy was looking at the landscape below them and really had no idea what the angel meant, so he decided to say the first thing that came to his mind. "Monument?"

"Right! You're a genius at guessing. We're on our way to a village lost in the jungle. Its symbol is a huge monument in the shape of a shield, carved out of wood, to recall all the men and women who defended their freedom, their faith, and their way of life."

"We're going to the jungle?"

"Yes, but don't worry – I'll watch out for any snakes there. I'll leave you beside the monument, and from there you'll go alone."

"And what language do the villagers speak?"

"Oh, don't worry about that! I'll provide an instant translation."

"Angel buddy, don't you get tired with so much work?"

It remains to be seen if angels get tired, because that's not part of our story. Within a minute, they had arrived at their destination. Jimmy found himself beneath a huge shield supported by the trunk of a massive tree. The tree itself looked like some great warrior that the shield protected.

Jimmy had the statue of the Infant Jesus with him, and he entrusted himself to him. "Dear Infant Jesus, I ask you again to come into the hearts of many people," he prayed as he kissed the statue. He breathed in the fresh, sweet-smelling air. It was a beautiful place, an earthly paradise.

He started to walk, but stopped suddenly as he saw some children running towards him. Their skin was dark, and they wore only shorts; they were barefoot, and they had some red lines of paint on their left arms. Jimmy was uneasy, even after all the assurances his guardian angel had given him. The children surrounded Jimmy, and he didn't know what to expect. But the only thing that happened is that one of the children put his hand on Jimmy's shoulders and said to him, "Hi! Why did you take so long?"

Jimmy looked at the child in surprise. *Did they know he was coming? Were they waiting for him?* Perhaps his outspoken com-

ment to the angel on their way to see Emily had had some good effect.

"You're Jimmy, right?"

Jimmy was now even more surprised, and his expression caused the children to laugh as they continued to gather around him.

"Yes, I'm Jimmy, and I've come to…"

"…to give us the statue of the Infant Jesus!"

"How do you know everything?"

"We'll tell you in the hut. Come on, or we'll be late!"

They ran around the wooden shield and headed into the jungle. Jimmy had a hard time keeping up with the boys, who jumped over tree roots and avoided branches and bushes easily.

"Come on, Jimmy!"

Jimmy was breathing hard – but happily, very happily. It was the first time he was able to run and play since beginning this Christmas adventure. This jungle was giving him an experience that he never thought he would have: the chance to celebrate Christmas with those who have no snow, sleds, or roaring fires – Christmas in the summertime! It seemed strange to him, but it was all very colorful and beautiful.

The jungle children stopped at the foot of a huge tree where there was enough room for everyone to sit on the tree's large roots and wait. Jimmy finally caught up with them.

"Tired?"

"No, no – but where are we going?"

"To the missionary's hut."

"The missionary? Was he the one who told you I was coming? Is he waiting for me?"

"Yes."

"Is it far?"

"No, it's just on the other side of the waterfall."

In fact, the sound of cascading water had been getting louder. It was a sound that blended with the chorus of the birds and the shrieks of the monkeys. Without another word, the children took off running again, and Jimmy hurried behind them so he wouldn't lose the trail.

They were in a hurry to bring him to the hut. They followed a path (that kept getting narrower) among the lush foliage, until Jimmy came to a hanging bridge that the others had already crossed. The bridge wasn't at all like the bridge in his village, which he flew over every day on his bicycle. This bridge was just a bunch of narrow pieces of wood supported by a tangle of ropes that were only waist high.

The bridge shook at every step. The children were shouting at him from the other side, and one of them, seeing Jimmy's difficulty, came towards him to give him a hand.

"Wow! Thanks!"

"You're welcome, Jimmy. Exciting, isn't it? We helped the missionary to build it."

"Good job! It's...a very handy way to cross the river."

The hut was nearby, and the children approached it slowly and silently. It was easy to see the respect they had for the missionary who shared his life with the villagers.

"Father John!" shouted one of them. Without waiting for an answer, they pushed aside the hanging reeds that formed the door of the hut. Jimmy went inside with them. Father John, the missionary, was an old priest with a white beard.

"Jimmy! A pleasure to meet you!" he said, giving Jimmy a big hug.

"Father John, I'm happy to meet you too."

"Please, sit down. How was the trip here?"

"Well, don't you know already?"

"I don't know everything, just what's necessary to know. The good Lord has allowed me to serve him in this beautiful jungle, and it has its advantages."

"Do you know what I have with me?"

"Oh, yes! Don't worry about explaining things to me. Instead, I should explain why we are so happy to see you."

The children had been listening silently, but their eyes followed everything attentively.

Suddenly, one of them interrupted. "Father John, will you tell him the story?"

"I certainly will," the priest replied.

The children clapped their hands with joy, and the youngest one told Jimmy that it was a very good story. The priest began to speak, holding in his hands the crucifix that hung around his neck.

"I came to this jungle forty years ago. I remember that a leopard was following me. I was very nervous, and when I saw the first huts of the village, I ran as fast as I could. The leopard could have caught me, but instead he kept his distance and watched me get away. The people welcomed me, and when they saw the leopard behind me, they thought that I was being protected by God. I had come to take over for another missionary who was too sick to work any more. It was easy to continue his work, because he had taught

the people very well. Thanks be to God, it was almost Christmas-time, and so it was my first big feast with the people. Since then, every year, we have prepared for Christmas with great love. Christ is born in the jungle!

"A few years later, the bishop came to visit us. As a gift, he brought us the little figures for our Nativity scene. You can't imagine how we thanked him! They are very special, and the people love them. Then, a little over a month ago, we discovered that the statue of the Infant Jesus had disappeared. What a commotion that caused in the village! The chief of the tribe ordered all of the huts to be searched. The statue was not found, so the men went off into the jungle to look for it, but there was no sign of it!

"Shortly after this, one night I woke up to a leopard growling. I was frightened at first, but then – I don't know why – I felt sure that it was not a threat, but a sign of something. I lit a torch and went out into the darkness. At that moment, I saw the wild animal, which reminded me of my first time coming to the village. We looked at each other, and then the leopard lowered his head, turned around, and began to walk away slowly.

"I followed him. I don't remember how many hours I walked. I could barely find my way. Then I tripped and fell. As I got up, I lit the torch again and saw that the leopard had climbed a tree. I looked up, and when I glanced down again, there in front of me was a young man dressed in white. He smiled and came towards me. We talked until dawn."

One of the children interrupted him. "You never told us who the young man was. I think it was St. John."

The children laughed, and the story continued.

"Yes, I didn't say who it was because it's not necessary. It's enough to say that I learned many things that night, and I found out what had happened to our statue of the Infant Jesus. It had been taken to the real Nativity cave to be blessed personally by the Holy Family, and I was told that a boy named Jimmy would bring it here to me today."

Jimmy felt a shiver pass through him as he was surrounded by the noisy children and the visible happiness of the missionary priest.

"Here's the statue. The Infant Jesus has come back to the jungle to be with his friends," Jimmy said, as he held out his hands to present the statue. The children all came to see it and, one by one, they all kissed the statue lovingly. Jimmy's own joy seemed to explode within him.

Then the missionary said to him: "I know that you're in a hurry. I just wanted you to know that this Christmas the Infant Jesus is going to shower special graces on our people. In particular, there are marriages that are going to be reconciled and two adults who will be baptized. They were children when I first came here!"

The children didn't realize that Jimmy had to leave right away.

"Father John, can't Jimmy stay with us? Didn't he come to be with us this Christmas?"

"Children, Jimmy came on behalf of the Holy Family to give us the statue of the Infant Jesus. I don't think that even he knows what he still has to do before returning home. And, to be fair, he has to be home in time for Christmas dinner and midnight Mass with his own family."

"Why don't you stay, Jimmy?" the children asked, pulling on his arms.

"I'd love to. By the way, what are your names?"

"You haven't told him your names?" asked the priest.

"Oops… we forgot! I'm Mark."

"I'm Stephen!"

"I'm Matthew."

"I'm Paul!"

Jimmy did have to leave right away. He knew that in a moment he would be flying through the sky. He hugged his new friends and told them he would ask the angel if he could visit them again.

Then he knelt down to ask for Father John's blessing. The other children also knelt down. The priest held up the statue of the Infant Jesus and blessed them all. Jimmy then stood up and hugged the old missionary, who said seriously, "Jimmy, can I ask you a favor?"

"Of course, Father John."

The missionary took him by the arm, and they moved a few steps away from the children. The old priest said quietly, "Tell our Lord that I thank him from the bottom of my heart for his infinite kindness and for all the good he has done for the people of this village."

"I will, Father."

"But please also tell him this, and don't forget: Tell him that I am now old; ask him to send a young priest to help me and then to take my place, in his good time. You know, I think one of these next Christmases I will be in heaven. I can't wait! Please tell him that we are praying for vocations, and we are praying that there will always be a priest in this village."

"I will be sure to pass on your message, Father John."

The missionary kissed Jimmy on the forehead, and Jimmy kissed his hands. Just then, they heard a leopard growl.

"Hey! This cat always seems to show up on time! I think he's come for you this time," the priest said.

"For *me*?" Jimmy asked, feeling a little scared.

They came out of the hut, but they didn't see any leopard. Only Jimmy saw his guardian angel on the wooden bridge.

Jimmy waved at everyone and took off running. The children followed him as far as the bridge. This time Jimmy ran over it confidently, at full speed. The angel told him to go a little ways into the jungle. Hidden from the others behind a wall of trees, the angel smiled at Jimmy and asked him, "Did you like my imitation of a leopard?"

Love Has No Limits

The trip back to the Nativity cave was a joyful one. The angel realized how content Jimmy was. "You're happy, aren't you?"

"Yes, I am! It's so great to be able to help others and to welcome the Infant Jesus at Christmas."

That was all they said. The boy rested on the angel's shoulder and watched the changing landscapes below. Each one was as beautiful as the other. He closed his eyes for a moment, and when he opened them, he was once again at the Nativity cave.

They went into the cave. This time the shepherds were there keeping the Holy Family company – the newborn baby, his holy

Mother, and St. Joseph. Jimmy approached them with his angel buddy, and they knelt down in adoration. After a few minutes St. Joseph motioned to them to draw closer, and he said, "Jimmy, thank you very much for all you have done for us."

"No, thank you all so much!"

The Virgin Mary touched the Infant Jesus' nose, and he smiled and took her finger in his hands. She looked sweetly at Jimmy and said to him, "My son, we are all very happy."

"I'm so happy to hear that, Mother."

"Jessica, Henry, Emily, their families, and Father John's villagers are all spending Christmas with us."

"I'm so glad to know them all!"

"You would have liked to spend more time with them, I know."

"Yes, very much…but I would also have liked to visit more and more families – millions of families – and knock on their doors this Christmas."

"You are a very good boy, Jimmy. And, in a way, you have done this, because love goes beyond where you are physically."

"Yes, I'm learning that."

"Good. It's time for you to return home now. I don't want your mother to be worried."

"There is one message from Father John…"

"Isn't he a holy priest? Yes, his daily prayer for vocations will be answered. Soon he will receive a visit from his bishop, and the bishop's own secretary will stay in the village to help him. Later, a young priest will be able to take his place."

"He will be very happy."

"Yes, he will. Pray every day for priests so that the Infant Jesus can be born all over the world."

As she was saying this, the Virgin Mary stood up with the Infant Jesus in her arms. Jimmy kissed him and left. St. Joseph accompanied him to the entrance of the cave, where he showed him again the leather bag.

"Can I give you some advice?" St. Joseph asked.

"Sure," replied Jimmy.

"Continue writing in your Christmas messages that you want to help bring the Infant Jesus to many hearts, and I promise you that we will see each other again. There are hundreds of families to visit!"

"I will – I promise!"

St. Joseph smiled and hugged Jimmy, and then he gave him an unusual gift. "I found this slingshot for you. There's a shepherd who makes very good ones, and I thought you would like to have a new one."

"Thank you!"

"It's got a good aim. Well, we'll see you again at your home."

A Statue for Jimmy's Family

The entire journey home was fun. Jimmy and his angel laughed, talked, and sang the whole time. When they came to the clearing in the woods, there was nothing left to say. In fact, they both knew that their friendship would continue on, as always, in total trust and confidence.

The angel went with Jimmy to the tree where he had left his bicycle. The boy got on his bicycle and sat for a moment, looking at his friend.

"What should I do now? Go and search for my friends, or go home?"

"You decide. It depends on the time."

"Of course!" Jimmy looked at his watch and was surprised to find that it was only three o'clock in the afternoon. "Did we do all that in one minute?"

In a modest and playful way, the angel answered, "I'd say we did it in half a minute. We were traveling really fast!"

"You're amazing, angel buddy!"

"I suggest you visit your friends so you can help Father Andrew finish the parish Nativity scene and prepare for midnight Mass."

"Okay."

"Or perhaps it would be better to go home first and give Henry's statue of the Infant Jesus to your mother. Or did you forget about it?"

"Oh, yes! You're right. Imagine giving a statue to everyone except my own family! They'll all be thrilled, and I'll tell them… What *will* I tell them?"

"Don't worry; I'll give you a few ideas. You'd better get going, because here on earth time flies by."

Jimmy began to pedal off on his bicycle, followed by his angel. As the forest path ended and the road to the village began, the angel flew off, and Jimmy felt a hand of encouragement on his back.

The boy raced back to the village, pedaling at full speed and humming a Christmas carol. Jimmy had fulfilled his Christmas wish, but only in part, because he wanted to continue fulfilling it every year.

Christmas is beautiful only when the Infant Jesus is born in the hearts of people – and when there is someone like Jimmy ready to make it happen.

Merry Christmas!